D0618366

First published in the United States
of America in 1990 by The Mallard Press

Mallard Press and its accompanying design
and logo are trademarks of BDD Promotional
Book Company, Inc.

Published by
Twin Books
15 Sherwood Place
Greenwich, CT 06830 USA

© 1990 The Walt Disney Company

All rights reserved.

ISBN 0-792-45370-0

Printed in Spain

Bedtime STORIES

Walt Disney Publications

Written by
Don Ferguson, Nikki Grimes, and Betty Birney

Illustrated by
Vaccaro Associates, Inc.
David Molina and Terry Shakespeare

Twin Books   **MALLARD PRESS**

Contents

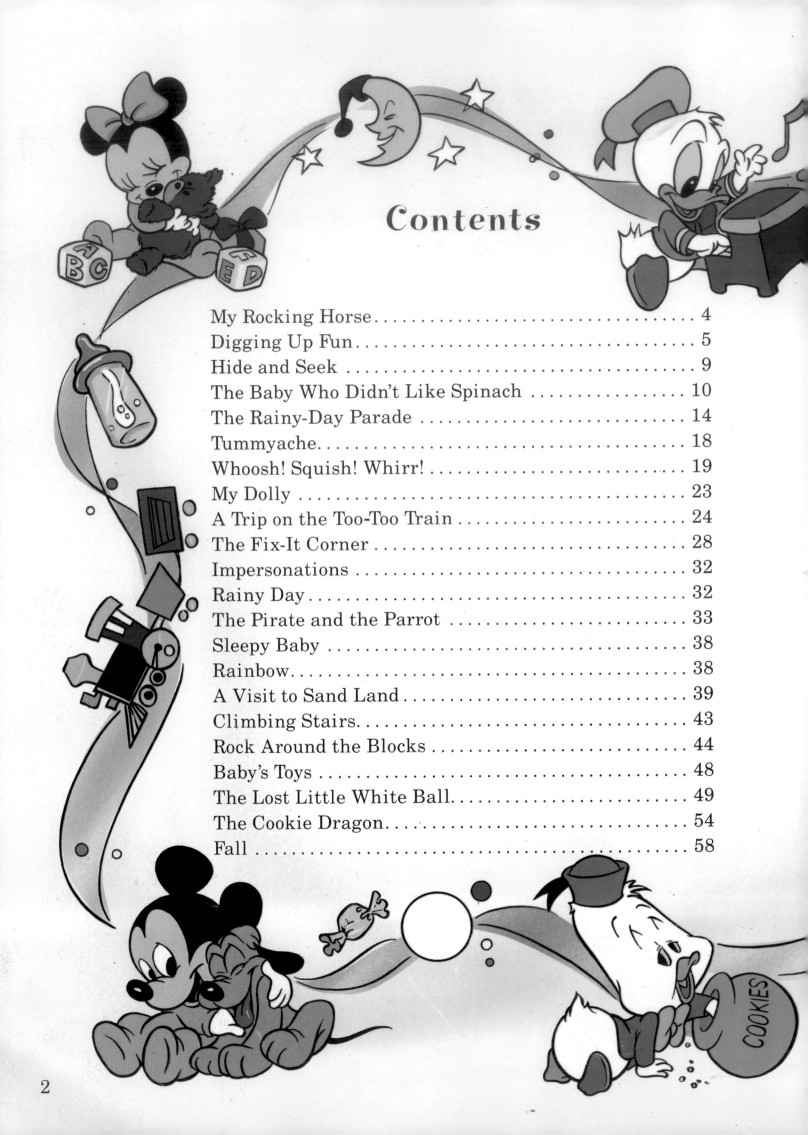

My Rocking Horse

Today we went a thousand miles,
　　My rocking horse and I,
To the land of purple crocodiles
　　Who live on pumpkin pie.

　　We went to where the lollipops
　　Grow wild in rows and rows.
We went to see the flippy-flop
　　Who walks upon his nose.

　　We went to where the bluebells chime,
　　And where the gingers snap.
And then we hurried home in time
　　For me to take my nap.

Digging up Fun

The day was warm and sunny. It was the kind of day that was perfect for playing in the sandbox.

What the Babies liked most about the sandbox was digging. Baby Mickey dug with a little spoon. Baby Daisy and Baby Goofy both used little shovels. Baby Minnie dug with a cup. And Baby Pluto dug with his paws.

Baby Minnie liked to build towering sandcastles. Baby Mickey liked to dig sand tunnels, while Baby Daisy enjoyed putting her handprints in the sand. Baby Goofy liked to make sand pies and sand cakes. They *looked* yummy enough to eat, but they tasted terrible. Baby Pluto made holes wherever his nose told him to.

On this particular day, Baby Minnie was digging a big hole, when suddenly she saw a glimpse of red.

"Look!" she shouted excitedly.

She dug and dug, and soon she dug up a big red bow.

"Mine!" said Baby Minnie, feeling proud.

Meanwhile, Baby Mickey took his little spoon and dug faster and faster until his spoon touched something hard. He dug some more, and soon he dug up a big blue block.

"Mine!" cried Baby Mickey, hugging the block.

Baby Daisy wished she could dig up something she could call her own, too. She turned over shovelful after shovelful of sand, until she uncovered something white. It was a white ball with a smiling face painted on it.

"Mine!" sighed Baby Daisy, holding her discovery tightly.

Baby Goofy hoped there would be something left in the sand for him to dig up. So he anxiously dug and dug with his little shovel. But all he dug up was a deep hole.

So Baby Goofy dug some more. This time he ended up with an even bigger hole.

Baby Goofy sighed. Baby Minnie had her red bow, Baby Mickey had his big blue block, and Baby Daisy had her round, smiling face. He just had to find something for himself!

Baby Goofy dug, and dug, and dug! Then he stopped to look into his hole, which was gigantic by now. Baby Goofy squealed with delight. Finally, in the middle of the hole, was something—a funny little hat.

"Mine!" said Baby Goofy, putting the funny little hat on top of his head.

The Disney Babies all played with their own toys, while Baby Pluto sat in the sand and scratched his ear.

After a while, Baby Mickey got tired of playing with his block. So he set it down in the sand. Then Baby Daisy got tired of playing with the smiling face. So she set it on top of the blue block.

Baby Minnie was tired of playing with the red bow, so she put it right between the block and the face. Then Baby Goofy took off the funny little hat and set it on top of the smiling face.

"Mine!" said Baby Minnie. What they had found were the pieces of a little toy clown she had lost. There was his blue block body, his round, smiling face, his red bow tie and his silly hat. "Mine, too," said Baby Mickey, Baby Daisy and Baby Goofy.

Suddenly Baby Pluto began to dig furiously, scattering sand all over the place.

"Stop!" shouted Baby Mickey.

But Baby Pluto wouldn't stop until he was ready. Then he stuck his head deep into the hole he had dug. The other Babies knew he had found something. Maybe it was another toy!

"Yip!" barked Baby Pluto. Then he turned toward the others with his find clutched between his jaws. What Baby Pluto had dug up was a bone!

All the other Disney Babies laughed. "Pluto's!" they agreed.

"Yip!" said Baby Pluto. Which, in doggy talk, means, "Mine!"

Hide and Seek

Close your eyes!
    Mustn't peek!
We are playing
    Hide and seek.

    Baby Donald
    Counts to ten.
Baby Mickey
    Hides again.

    "Hooray! I've found you!"
    Donald cheers.
"You forgot
    To hide your ears!"

The Baby Who
Didn't Like Spinach

Once upon a time, there was a Baby who didn't like spinach. His name was Baby Horace. Whenever his mother gave him spinach for dinner, Baby Horace would throw it out the cottage window.

"Spinach is good for you, Baby Horace!" his mother tried to explain. But Baby Horace kept throwing spinach away.

One day, right after Baby Horace had thrown his spinach out the window, a little man with big ears and a long, pointy nose appeared at the open window.

"Who threw that spinach at me?" he said, quite angrily, for bits of spinach were dangling from his ears and from his long, pointy nose.

10

But when he saw Baby Horace, he smiled. "Oh," he laughed. "It was *you*, was it?"

The little man was a troll. He lived in the forest all by himself. He was lonely, and had always wanted to have someone to play with.

"I see you don't like spinach," the troll said to Baby Horace. "I don't like it much, myself. If you come and live with me, I promise you'll never again have to eat spinach."

That sounded pretty good to Baby Horace, so he climbed out of his high chair and followed the troll into the woods.

Baby Horace and the troll played together all afternoon, and had lots of fun. When it was dinnertime, they went to the troll's cottage. The troll went to his cupboard and brought two big bowls of hay to the table.

"Yum, yum!" said the troll, munching on his leafy, green hay.

Baby Horace eagerly tried a mouthful of hay. It tasted even worse than spinach, and was all stickery, too. So he threw his bowl of hay out the window.

The troll was very surprised. "You don't like hay?" he said. "But that's what trolls like more than anything in the world!"

The next day, the troll and Baby Horace played all day in the troll's back yard. When dinnertime came again, the baby and the troll went into the cottage.

"Well, if you don't like hay," the troll said to Baby Horace, "we'll try something else." And the troll went to his cupboard and brought two mud pies to the table.

"Yum, yum!" said the troll, licking the mud from his lips.

Baby Horace tried a mouthful of the mud pie. It tasted worse than spinach! Even worse than hay!

So Baby Horace threw his mud pie out the cottage window.

"I never saw such a picky eater!" said the troll angrily. "You don't like hay, and you don't like mud pies! Whatever am I going to feed you?"

The troll paced the floor. Baby Horace watched, getting hungrier and hungrier. He started to cry.

"That does it!" said the troll. He grabbed Baby Horace and marched off to the village. He stomped straight up to Baby Horace's house and banged on the front door.

When Baby Horace's mother opened the door, in tears, the troll handed Baby Horace to her and said, "Here! Take him back! I won't have a picky eater living with me!"

Baby Horace's mother dried her tears. She was ever so glad to have her baby back home again. And the next time she made spinach for dinner, what do you think happened?

Why, Baby Horace ate it up, every bit. And never again did he throw anything out the window!

The Rainy-Day Parade

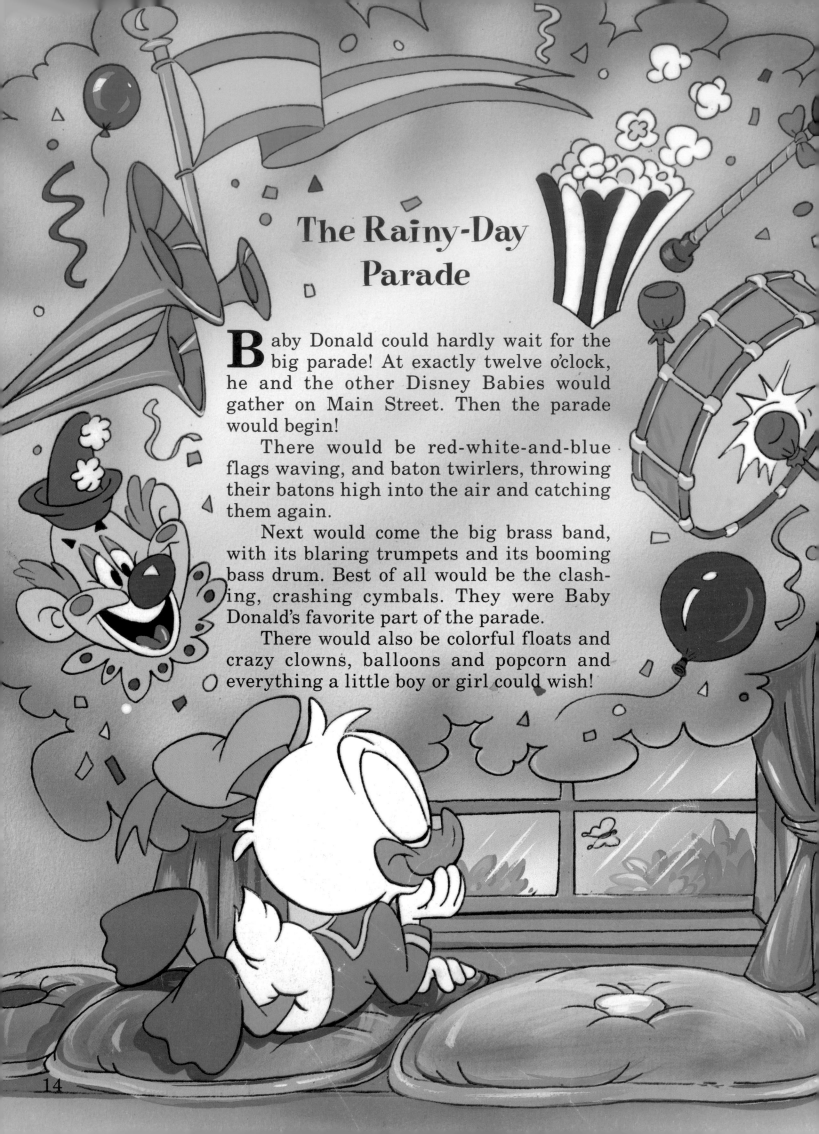

Baby Donald could hardly wait for the big parade! At exactly twelve o'clock, he and the other Disney Babies would gather on Main Street. Then the parade would begin!

There would be red-white-and-blue flags waving, and baton twirlers, throwing their batons high into the air and catching them again.

Next would come the big brass band, with its blaring trumpets and its booming bass drum. Best of all would be the clashing, crashing cymbals. They were Baby Donald's favorite part of the parade.

There would also be colorful floats and crazy clowns, balloons and popcorn and everything a little boy or girl could wish!

But when eleven o'clock came, a terrible thing happened. It began to rain. There was lightning and thunder, and the rain poured down. By twelve o'clock, Baby Donald knew that there would be no big parade today. So he went off to his room, feeling grumpy and disappointed.

A little later, Baby Donald heard a loud crash, then a clatter. Then he heard a *rat-a-tat-tat* and a *boom-boom-boom*. Baby Donald followed the sounds to the kitchen.

There was Baby Daisy, waving a big red-white-and-blue flag. The flag was really a red-white-and-blue towel, but the way Baby Daisy waved it, it looked a lot like a flag.

Right behind Baby Daisy was Baby Minnie, twirling a long wooden spoon round and round. She threw it into the air. When it came down again, Baby Minnie didn't quite catch it. Baby Donald laughed and clapped.

Ta-ra-ra-ra! Baby Mickey was blowing into a cardboard tube. *Toot-toot-toot!* Baby Clarabelle did the same.

Boom-boom! Baby Horace beat a cooking pot with two spoons. What a lovely noise it made!

Baby Goofy pretended to be a clown by making funny faces and acting silly.

It was the best parade Baby Donald had ever seen, but something was missing. And Baby Donald knew just what it was.

Crash! Bang! Boom! Bong!

Baby Daisy dropped her red-white-and-blue flag. Baby Minnie's spoon clattered to the floor. Baby Mickey, Baby Horace and Baby Clarabelle dropped their musical instruments, as well. Even Baby Goofy stopped making funny faces.

Boom! Crash! Bang! Bong! The noise got louder and louder.

Crash! Bash! Bong! Bang!

In the middle of the kitchen floor sat Baby Donald, banging two pot lids together, just as if they were cymbals.

The other Disney Babies cheered. Then they joined in. And even though it was raining outside, Baby Donald knew that this was the grandest parade they had ever seen! And the best part was, it was a parade they could have any time they wanted.

17

Tummyache

I only ate an apple.
And then I ate a plum.
Of course, there was that piece of cake,
No bigger than a crumb.

Oh, yes—those five bananas
And, maybe, a grape or three.
But, after all, my mother says
That fruit is good for me.

I could have skipped the pudding,
And the gumdrops were too sweet.
Okay! All right! I'll say it—
I had too much to eat!

Whoosh! Squish! Whirr!

It was a beautiful day in the park. Baby Mickey went up and down on the swings. He went swooshing down the slide. And he rocked back and forth on the rocking horse. But Baby Mickey was lonely. None of his friends had come to the park with him.

Then he heard a funny sound. *Whoosh, Whoosh!*

"What's that?" Baby Mickey wondered. Maybe *whoosh, whoosh!* was somebody to play with.

Suddenly Baby Mickey felt drops of water on his head. But it wasn't raining. In fact, the sun was shining brightly. But Baby Mickey was getting very wet.

Whoosh, whoosh!

Baby Mickey slid off the swing. The drops were coming from the sprinkler, which was watering the green, green grass.

Just then, Baby Mickey heard another funny sound. *Squish! Squish!*

"What's that?" Baby Mickey wondered. Maybe *squish, squish!* was somebody to play with.

Baby Mickey looked toward the sound, but all he saw was mud. His fingers were wiggling in the mud, and they were making the funny sound. *Squish, squish!* It felt good to wiggle his fingers in the mud. *Squish, squish, squish!*

But now Baby Mickey heard a different sound. *Whirr, whirr!*

Baby Mickey hurried toward the sound. Surely this time he would find somebody to play with.

Whirr, whirr!

But when he looked around, Baby Mickey saw a great, big lawn mower.

Baby Mickey knew that he could not play with a lawn mower. So he decided to investigate some more. And soon *he* made a funny sound.

"Ha, ha!" laughed Baby Mickey as he rolled around and around in the grass clippings which the lawnmower had left behind. Because of all the mud, the clippings stuck to Baby Mickey. He looked like he was covered with green fur. And that made Baby Mickey laugh even harder. "Ha, ha, ha!"

Snrr, Snrr!

"What's that?" thought Baby Mickey. He looked around to see where the funny noise was coming from.

Soon he found Baby Goofy taking a nap under a tree.

Snrr, snrr! Baby Goofy was snoring. He was sound asleep.

"Someone to play with!" thought Baby Mickey. "Someone who is lots of fun."

Snrr, snrr! Baby Goofy snored some more.

"Boo!" cried Baby Mickey.

Baby Goofy's eyes opened wide, and when he looked up, he saw a furry monster, covered with green hair.

"Help!" yelled Baby Goofy.

The furry, green-haired monster giggled. It was Baby Mickey! When Baby Goofy saw who it was, he laughed, too.

Now Baby Mickey had someone to play with. Soon Baby Goofy was rolling in the mud and the grass clippings with his friend.

Later that day, Baby Mickey and Baby Goofy heard another funny sound.

Splish, splash!

This time, they didn't have to investigate. They were in the bathtub, washing away all the mud and grass.

"Hee, hee!" laughed Baby Goofy as he splashed his friend.

"Hee, hee!" chuckled Baby Mickey, splashing Baby Goofy back.

And he didn't even mind taking a bath, as long as he had someone to play with.

My Dolly

My dolly walks.
My dolly talks.
My dolly laughs and cries.

She wears a bib.
She shares my crib.
At night, I close her eyes.

My dolly's hair
Grows down to there.
I comb it now and then.

My dolly's fun.
I have just one.
But you are my best friend!

A Trip on the Too-Too Train

Baby Goofy and Baby Clarabelle were so excited. At last they would get to ride on the little red and blue, Baby-sized train!

"Choo-choo!" cried Baby Clarabelle.

"Too-too!" added Baby Goofy. He couldn't quite say, "Choo-choo!"

The conductor walked past the Babies. "Tickets, please," he said.

Baby Clarabelle gave him her ticket. But Baby Goofy began to cry. If the conductor took his ticket away, how could he ride the train?

"Now, now," said the conductor. "If you're going to ride on the train, you must give me your ticket."

Baby Goofy stopped crying and handed his ticket to the conductor. "Too-too?" asked Baby Goofy.

The conductor nodded. "That's right," he said. "Choo-choo."

Soon the engineer climbed into the open car at the front of the train. "All aboard!" he called.

He pulled the rope on the bell. *Ring-a-ding-dong!*

He pulled the rope on the shiny brass whistle. Toot-toot!

And the train began to move. *Chug-a, chug-a, chug-a, chug-a!*

The train chugged around a curve and passed a fence where other children were waving. *Ring-a-ding-dong!* went the bell.

The train passed a field where ponies and donkeys were grazing. Toot-toot! went the whistle.

The train continued over a rickety-rackety bridge.

Clackety-clack-clack! went the train wheels.

Then the train headed for a small western town. There were cowboys standing out in the street.

"Yahoo!" shouted one of the cowboys, waving his hat.

"Too-too!" Baby Goofy shouted back to the cowboy.

Baby Goofy wanted to ride forever, round and round the park past the children, the ponies and the donkeys, through the tunnel and over the bridge, around the curve and through the old western town, round and round without stopping!

But the train was slowing down, and all too soon it stopped at the station. Baby Goofy didn't want to stop. And he certainly didn't want to get off the train.

"Boo-hoo!" cried Baby Goofy.

The conductor walked around the train. "Tickets, please," he said.

"Go! Go!" said Baby Goofy.

"We have to give others a chance to ride the train, too," said the conductor.

Baby Goofy sniffled. "Too-too," he said softly.

"I'm sorry," said the conductor, "but you can't ride without another ticket."

Suddenly a nice, familiar face appeared. It was Baby Mickey, and he had brought three tickets, one for himself, one for Baby Clarabelle, and one for Baby Goofy.

"Hi!" said Baby Goofy, taking the ticket from Baby Mickey.

"Hi!" said Baby Mickey.

Then the engineer pulled the rope on the big bell. *Ring-a-ding-dong!*

He pulled the rope on the shiny brass whistle. Toot-toot!

And the train began to move. *Chug-a-chug-chug!*

"Too-too!" cried Baby Goofy.

"Too-too!" said Baby Mickey.

"Me, too-too!" giggled Baby Clarabelle.

And the train started off on another adventure. It was even more wonderful than the first one, because Baby Goofy now had *two* friends to share his train ride.

27

The Fix-It Corner

Baby Clarabelle was becoming quite a nuisance. She just didn't understand that Baby Horace had a very important job, and was much too busy to play with her.

Baby Clarabelle really liked Baby Horace a lot. She thought he was very cute, and she was always creeping over to his Fix-It Corner and trying to get him to pay attention to her. She would grab his arm, or throw her big blue ball at him.

But Baby Horace had no time for silly games. He always had too much important work to do. Why, if it weren't for Baby Horace, nothing would ever get fixed! Hadn't he fixed Baby Donald's dump truck when the dumper got stuck? And who else could have fixed Baby Goofy's toy piano after Baby Goofy sat on it and broke his B-flat?

What was the matter with Baby Clarabelle? Why did she keep bopping him with that stupid big blue ball? Couldn't she see that he was busy? Why, he was the only Baby who could fix all the other Babies' broken toys!

It never occurred to Baby Horace that all Baby Clarabelle wanted was to play with him.

One rainy Tuesday afternoon, Baby Horace was in his Fix-It Corner, as usual, banging away at a broken top with his rubber hammer. All of a sudden, he heard Baby Minnie start to cry.

In just a moment, Baby Minnie was in Baby Horace's Fix-It Corner, clutching her teddy bear, and still crying. In fact, Baby Minnie was crying so hard that her tears were getting Teddy's ears wet.

Baby Horace took one look at Teddy and knew why Baby Minnie was in tears. Teddy had split a seam down his tummy, and his stuffing was popping out.

This was a real emergency! Teddy had to be fixed at once, before he lost all his stuffing!

Unfortunately, Baby Horace had never fixed a teddy bear before. First, he tried fixing Teddy with his rubber hammer. That didn't work. Then he tried his plastic screwdriver. Nope. That didn't work, either.

One by one, Baby Horace tried all his Fix-It tools. None of them would fix the broken bear. Time was running out for Teddy, just like his stuffing.

And Baby Minnie was still crying.

At last Baby Clarabelle crawled over to Baby Horace's Fix-It Corner to see what was going on. When she saw Baby Horace trying to fix Baby Minnie's teddy bear with a wooden monkey wrench, she giggled.

"Just like a boy," she thought to herself, and she went quickly to her own toy box.

In a minute, Baby Clarabelle was back, carrying her toy sewing basket. Wasting no time at all, she picked up Teddy and sewed up his seam. Soon Baby Minnie's teddy bear was as good as new!

Well, when Baby Horace saw what a good little fixer Baby Clarabelle turned out to be, he made a place for her in his Fix-It Corner.

From that day on, Baby Clarabelle fixed the girl babies' toys, and Baby Horace fixed the boy babies' toys.

And because there were now two fixers, Baby Horace and Baby Clarabelle had plenty of time to play with the beautiful blue ball.

31

Impersonations

Look! I'm a dog! "Bow-wow!"
I'm a cat when I go "meow!"
    When I "tweet," I sound very
    Much like a canary!
And "bloop!" I'm a goldfish now!

Rainy Day

The drops tap my windows,
    The wind bumps my doors.
It's raining on my house.
    Is it raining on yours?

I'm warm by the fireplace,
    All safely indoors.
It's cozy in my house.
    Is it cozy in yours?

The Pirate and the Parrot

Pirate's Cove." That's what the sign read. An old legend said that pirates had buried a chest full of treasure on the beach many years ago.

Baby Donald and Baby Daisy spent the whole day digging away with their little shovels. Baby Donald dug up an old shoe, a piece of seaweed and lots of little sand crabs. Baby Daisy dug up two pink shells and a shiny black rock. But they both wished they could find the pirate treasure chest. Suddenly, Baby Donald's shovel hit something hard.

"Ooh!" said Baby Donald.

"Aah!" said Baby Daisy.

The two of them dug as fast as they could, and soon uncovered a very old chest

"Whee!" said Baby Donald.

Baby Daisy reached over to open the treasure chest.

"Stop right there, matey!" a deep voice called out.

Baby Donald and Baby Daisy looked up, and up—and up! Standing right in front of them was a very tall, very mean-looking pirate! He wore a black hat with a broad brim and a red feather, a black coat, shiny red pants and black shoes with huge gold buckles. Around his waist was a blue and red sash, and over one eye was a shiny black patch.

"Stop! Stop!" squawked a bright green parrot which was sitting on the pirate's shoulder.

"Looks like you found yourself some treasure, landlubbers," the pirate's voice boomed out.

"Lubbers!" repeated the parrot.

"*My* treasure," added the pirate.

"Oops!" Baby Donald swallowed hard. Baby Daisy's eyes grew very round.

"After all, this is Pirate's Cove. And *I* am a pirate. So this must the treasure I buried many years ago."

"Mine! Mine!" squawked the parrot, flapping his wings.

"I'll be checking it all, to see that you haven't taken anything," said the pirate, as he bent down and slowly opened the treasure chest.

Creak! went the lid. The chest was very old.

"Well, I'll be!" exclaimed the pirate as he gazed down at the treasure. "It's all here, just as I remembered it."

"Here! Here! All here!" the parrot announced.

Baby Donald and Baby Daisy leaned over to look. They could hardly wait to see the sparkling jewels and gold coins.

But that's not what they saw, at all. Instead of priceless treasure, all they saw were beach toys and a big, round beach ball.

"Yes, just as I remember hiding them here when I was a lad," said the pirate with a big smile on his face.

"Catch!" He tossed the ball to Baby Donald. Baby Donald giggled and threw the ball to Baby Daisy. She laughed and threw the ball back to the pirate.

"Shiver me timbers, this is fun!" said the pirate, throwing the ball high into the air.

"Fun!" echoed the parrot.

Baby Donald and Baby Daisy played catch with the pirate until it was time to leave.

"Wait, mateys! You mustn't leave yet!"

Baby Donald and Baby Daisy didn't know what the pirate was talking about.

"We can't leave treasure like this sitting around Pirate's Cove. We have to hide it for the next time we come back to play."

"Play! Play!" squawked the green parrot.

Soon the three of them had buried the treasure chest again.

"Next time, I won't wait so long to come back," said the pirate, shaking the Babies' hands.

"Just remember, mateys—the best treasures on earth are friends to have fun with," the pirate told them. "Good-bye, now."

"Bye! Bye!" shouted the parrot.

"Bye! Bye!" shouted Baby Donald and Baby Daisy. And as they started home, they were already thinking about their next trip to Pirate's Cove.

Sleepy Baby

In winter, some get up
        At night,
And dress by yellow
        Candlelight.

But winter, summer, spring
        Or fall,
He'd rather not get up
        At all!

Rainbow

At the end of every rainbow
        (As I've frequently been told),
At the end of every rainbow
        There's a pot of shining gold.

But when I look up in the sky
        And see a rainbow bend,
I cannot help but wonder why
        They never say which end!

A Visit to Sand Land

Baby Mickey yawned. He felt warm and cozy, tucked in his bed. Still, he didn't want to go to sleep, so even though his eyelids felt heavy, he tried to keep his eyes wide open.

"Hurry up! Go to sleep!" said a low, gravelly voice. Baby Mickey saw a roly-poly little man seated at the foot of his bed.

"You're expected, you know. Now, come along!" said the man, as he rose and shook himself all over. Tiny grains of sand flew everywhere. "I'm the Sandman," said the little man. "Come along! Don't drag your feet. Come with me to Sand Land."

As soon as Baby Mickey grabbed the hand that the Sandman held out, the two of them flew off through the clouds, faster than planes, faster than birds, even faster than the wind.

All too soon, the Sandman swooped down and the two of them landed on the sand with a thud. Everything was sand, in every direction. And right next to them was the biggest sandcastle Baby Mickey had ever seen.

"Don't dilly-dally," said the Sandman, smiling. "It's almost time for our dinner."

Quick as a wink, the Sandman led Baby Mickey across the sand bridge, right over the sand moat and into the great sand hall, which led into the sand dining room. Baby Mickey sat down at a long table.

The other guests—all sand people except for Baby Mickey—were friendly and jolly, like the Sandman, but Baby Mickey didn't like the sand food very much.

After dinner, the Sandman invited Baby Mickey outside to play. "Our sand is your sand," he said with a wave of his hand. Baby Mickey did like playing in the sand, and he quickly built a little sand figure. It looked just like a snowman. But, unlike any other snowman Baby Mickey had seen, this figure came to life!

"Hi! I'm Sandy," the figure said in a squeaky voice.

For hours, Sandy and Baby Mickey giggled and played tag and hide-and-seek. Suddenly a whistle blew. Mickey turned around and saw the Sandman.

"Time to go to work," he said.

Then the Sandman told Sandy and Baby Mickey to build a sand mountain. It was hard work, making a mound of sand grow into a hill of sand, and then into a mountain. But once it was finished, the Sandman said, "Well done. Now it's time to play again!"

Sandy taught Baby Mickey how to start at the top of the mountain and roll all the way to the bottom. Then they crawled back to the top and rolled down again. Baby Mickey thought that Sand Land was a very strange place, but it was mostly lots of fun.

Then the wind began to blow, first softly, then harder and harder, until the sand was blowing off the side of the mountain. Sand swirled around Baby Mickey and Sandy and blew them right off the ground.

"Stop!" cried Baby Mickey, holding onto Sandy.

The sand made his eyes itch. He rubbed them, but that made them itch even more. He blinked hard, then opened his eyes again. And to his great surprise, he was back in his own bed.

Baby Mickey sighed. Maybe it had all been a dream, and there was no Sandman, at all.

He sat up in bed and rubbed his eyes again. A few tiny grains of sand floated down onto his blanket.

It wasn't a dream! He could see the Sandman again, whenever he went to sleep. But right now, Baby Mickey was glad to be in his own bed, in his own home. He knew that a bowl of sand wasn't nearly as yummy as the breakfast he could smell cooking in his own kitchen.

Climbing Stairs

Here we are,
    Halfway there,
Resting on
    The middle stair.

It's been so long
    Since we began,
I've quite forgot—
    What was our plan.

Can you tell me,
    Little pup—
Are we climbing
    Down...or up?

Rock Around the Blocks

Baby Donald had the biggest set of blocks in the neighborhood. He loved to build skyscrapers out of blocks and tried to make each skyscraper taller than the one before.

One day Baby Horace, Baby Clarabelle and Baby Goofy came to visit. They watched Baby Donald make a row of blue and white blocks. On top of that, he carefully stacked a row of red and green blocks. The next row was pink and purple, and on top of that was a row of yellow and orange blocks.

Then he started all over again. There were blue and white blocks, red and green blocks, pink and purple blocks, ending with yellow and orange blocks.

Soon the skyscraper was even taller than Baby Donald.

"Look!" said Baby Donald.

"Ooh!" said Baby Clarabelle.

"Ahhh!" said Baby Horace.

"Whee!" said Baby Goofy. He crawled toward the skyscraper and accidentally knocked against it.

First the skyscraper tipped to one side. Then it swayed all the way over to the other side. Finally, the whole thing came tumbling down, block by block. "Boo-hoo!" cried Baby Donald. He was mad that Baby Goofy had knocked over his skyscraper. He was also sad.

Baby Goofy was sorry, and he tried to set the skyscraper up again. First, he made a row of blue and green blocks.

"No!" shouted Baby Donald.

Next, Baby Goofy made a row of pink and yellow blocks.

"No, no, no!" shouted Baby Donald.

Then Baby Goofy stacked a row of purple and orange blocks.

"No, no, no, no, no!!" shouted Baby Donald, banging the floor with his fists. He did not think a skyscraper should look like that at all! Then he bumped up and down so hard that Baby Goofy's skyscraper came tumbling down!

Baby Goofy started to laugh, and that made Baby Donald so mad that he crawled right out of the room.

Baby Horace, Baby Clarabelle and Baby Goofy didn't think there was just one way to build a sky-scraper. And they didn't think a skyscraper was the only thing you could build with blocks. So while Baby Donald was pouting, they began to build again.

But Baby Horace didn't build a skyscraper. He built a road where he could drive toy cars and trucks.

Baby Clarabelle built a corral for her toy animals.

And Baby Goofy built a pyra-mid, with five blocks on the bot-tom, then a row of four, a row of three, a row of two, and one block on the very top.

When Baby Donald came back into the room, expecting to see a skyscraper, he was very surprised. But he wasn't mad, and he wasn't sad.

"Ooh! Ahh! Whee!" said Baby Donald, admiring the block buildings. Then, with a swoop of his hand, he knocked them all down.

Baby Horace, Baby Clarabelle and Baby Goofy felt mad and sad that Baby Donald had knocked down their buildings.

Then Baby Donald began to laugh. Baby Goofy began to laugh, too, and Baby Horace and Baby Clarabelle chuckled right along with them.

"Look!" said Baby Donald as he began to stack blocks again. His friends joined in, and soon they built a huge block castle, with a tower and a moat. They used every single block, and they all admired it very much, especially when Baby Clarabelle put a flag on top.

"Ooh!" said Baby Clarabelle.

"Ahh!" said Baby Horace.

"Whee!" said Baby Donald and Baby Goofy.

Then they knocked the block castle down and started all over again.

Baby's Toys

A baby's toys
Make lots of noise.
They honk, or quack, or ding.

Some, on wheels,
Make squeaks and squeals
When Baby pulls the string.

Some sound chimes,
Or nursery rhymes.
Some tweet just like a bird.

That's why I love
My baseball glove.
It never says a word!

The Lost Little White Ball

Baby Mickey and Baby Minnie were having a wonderful time visiting the farm. They had already had a pony ride. They had fed the ducks on the pond. They had ridden in the haywagon. Now they sat under a shade tree, playing a game of catch with a little white ball.

"Whee!" said Baby Minnie, rolling the ball to Baby Mickey.

Baby Mickey bounced the ball back to Baby Minnie. "Uh-oh," he said as the ball bounced away from Baby Minnie and out of sight.

Baby Mickey and Baby Minnie had to find the ball if they wanted to keep playing their game.

First they looked in the vegetable garden. They saw bright orange carrots, leafy green lettuce, and big red tomatoes. But they did not see the little white ball.

Baby Mickey and Baby Minnie decided to look in the big red barn. There they saw a big brown cow, munching hay in a stall.

"Mooo!" said the cow.

"Moo!" said Baby Mickey.

"Moo!" said Baby Minnie.

Next to the cow was a bucket of fresh, white milk. But there was no little white ball.

Next Baby Mickey and Baby Minnie visited the pigpen.

"Oink, oink, oink!" said the pretty pink pigs.

Baby Minnie giggled and tried to say "Oink, oink" back. Big pigs and little pigs were all rolling around in the mud. There was lots of mud, but there was no little white ball in the pigpen.

Then Baby Mickey saw the rooster sitting on the fence.

"Cock-a-doodle-doo!" crowed the rooster.

The rooster had a bright red comb on top of his head. But he did not have a little white ball.

"Ne-e-e-eigh!" Baby Minnie saw the pony in his stall. Farmer Jones, who was brushing the pony, let Baby Minnie feed the pony some sugar. The pony licked Baby Minnie's hand and she giggled. But Baby Minnie did not find the little white ball.

"Ba-a-a-ah!"

Baby Mickey and Baby Minnie both turned and saw the old billy goat in the barnyard. Farmer Jones saw him, too.

"I hope old Billy didn't find your ball," said Farmer Jones. "Because that old goat will eat anything!"

"Uh-oh," thought Baby Mickey. He was afraid he and Baby Minnie would never be able to play catch with the little white ball again!

51

"Cluck, cluck!"

"Well, well! Maybe our friend Henrietta can help you," suggested Farmer Jones.

Baby Mickey, Baby Minnie and Farmer Jones hurried over to the henhouse. It was just like a regular house on the outside, but much smaller. Inside there were rows and rows of nests, with chickens sitting on them.

"Cluck, cluck!" said Henrietta from her nest.

"Cluck, cluck, cluck!" answered Baby Mickey.

But he didn't see the little white ball. Baby Mickey and Baby Minnie both felt sad as they started to leave the henhouse.

"Wait just a second," said Farmer Jones. "I think Henrietta is trying to tell us something."

"Cluck, cluck!" said the red hen.

"Do you have something for us?" asked the farmer. Then he reached into Henrietta's nest and pulled out something round and white.

"Egg?" asked Baby Mickey.

"Egg!" said Baby Minnie.

"Not an egg," said Farmer Jones. "I don't think Henrietta laid this, do you?"

Farmer Jones held out the little white ball.

"Hooray!" shouted Baby Mickey.

"Hooray!" cried Baby Minnie.

"Cluck, cluck!" said Henrietta, flapping her wings.

Then Baby Mickey and Baby Minnie hurried outside to play catch with their little white ball.

The Cookie Dragon

Once upon a time, there was a town where nobody knew how to make cookies. That was because cookies hadn't been invented yet; nobody had ever heard of them. So when children came in from play, their mothers would give them broccoli and milk, instead of cookies and milk.

Outside the town, in a dark forest, lived a dragon named Spot. Because the people in the town were afraid of dragons, no one ever visited Spot. He was a very lonely dragon, but he tried to keep from feeling sorry for himself by inventing things.

One day Spot was trying to think of something he would like to invent, when he suddenly thought of cookies. He immediately went to his kitchen and whipped up a batch of cookies. Then he popped them into his oven.

The wonderful smell of the baking cookies drifted out from Spot's cave and through the forest, until it reached the noses of the townspeople.

The smell smelled so delicious that they all stopped whatever they were doing and sniffed.

"Mmmmm!" they said. "What is that dragon doing that smells so awfully good?"

But they were so afraid of the dragon that they wouldn't go into the forest to find out.

The only person in town who wasn't afraid of the dragon was a Baby named Gus. Baby Gus was always too busy eating and sleeping to be afraid of anything.

When the lovely smell of Spot's baking drifted under Baby Gus's nose, he woke up from his nap and sniffed. He climbed out of his crib and began to creep into the woods, following the delicious smell.

Now, people always said that Baby Gus had the best nose in town for sniffing out good things to eat. Sure enough, in no time at all, Baby Gus had sniffed out something good to eat—in Spot's cave.

The dragon was just taking his cookies out of the oven when Baby Gus appeared. Spot was so surprised to have a visitor that he jumped and said, "Yeow!"

But Baby Gus paid no attention to the dragon. He went straight to the cookies cooling on Spot's table and helped himself to one.

Meanwhile, back in town, people soon discovered that Baby Gus had disappeared.

"It's that delicious smell," said the mayor. "He's gone into the forest to follow it."

"Oh, I knew it was one of the dragon's tricks," said the police chief. "He wanted to lure one of us to his cave, and now he's done it."

"We must save Baby Gus from the dragon," the mayor said.

And even though they were afraid of the dragon, the townspeople gathered up their courage and went off to rescue Baby Gus.

When they arrived at Spot's cave, they were amazed to find Baby Gus and the dragon sitting at the kitchen table, having milk and strange-looking round things.

When the townspeople found out what a nice person the dragon was, and how delicious his cookies were, they invited Spot to come to town and make cookies for them every day.

Of course Spot agreed, because he had been so lonesome, all by himself in the forest.

And Baby Gus? Well, he ate happily ever after, which was what he liked to do best, next to sleeping, of course.

Fall

The leaves turn red and gold
When Fall is in the air.
The wind picks up the leaves
And blows them here and there.

I gather up the leaves
And make a nice, neat stack.
But the wind blows them away again,
Soon as I turn my back!

The Piano

The piano is one of life's joys.
It's one of my favorite toys.
   Though my fingers can't yet
   Play a Bach minuet,
My fists make a wonderful noise!

The Ladybug's Tale

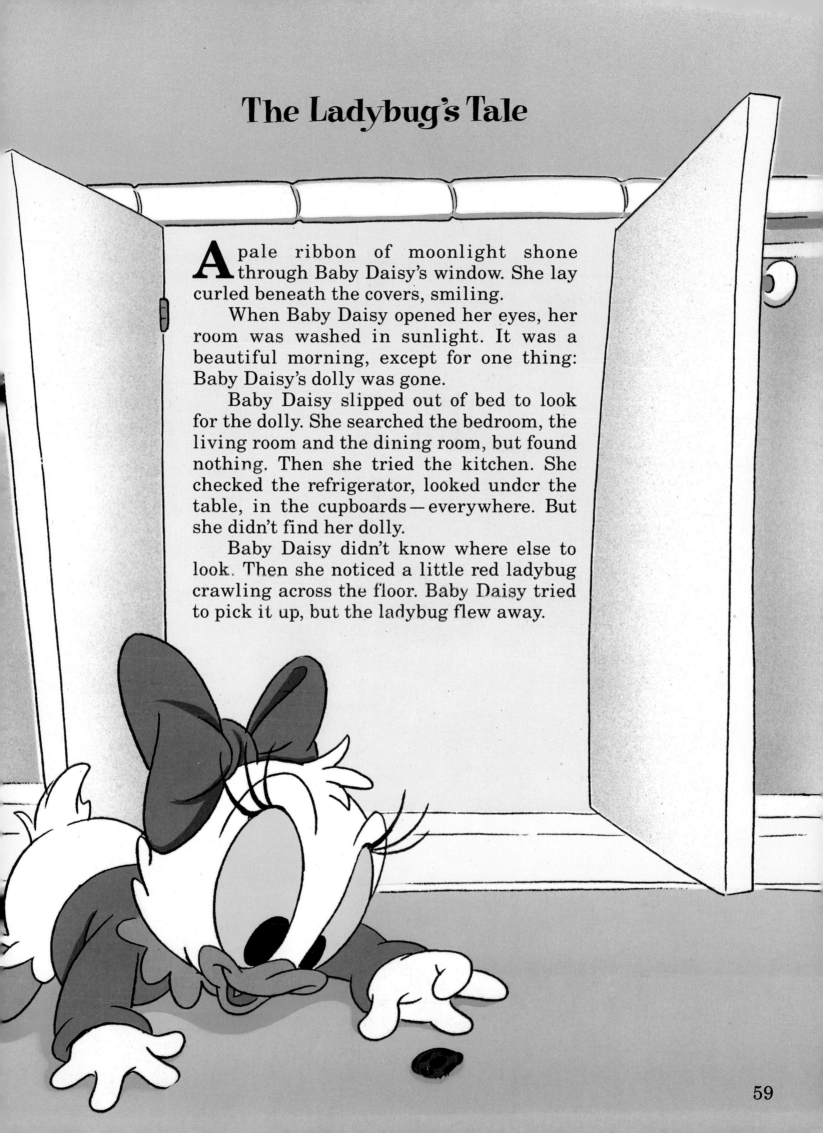

A pale ribbon of moonlight shone through Baby Daisy's window. She lay curled beneath the covers, smiling.

When Baby Daisy opened her eyes, her room was washed in sunlight. It was a beautiful morning, except for one thing: Baby Daisy's dolly was gone.

Baby Daisy slipped out of bed to look for the dolly. She searched the bedroom, the living room and the dining room, but found nothing. Then she tried the kitchen. She checked the refrigerator, looked under the table, in the cupboards—everywhere. But she didn't find her dolly.

Baby Daisy didn't know where else to look. Then she noticed a little red ladybug crawling across the floor. Baby Daisy tried to pick it up, but the ladybug flew away.

"Don't!" snapped the ladybug.

"Oh!" said Daisy, surprised. She'd never met a talking ladybug.

"Now, what on earth were you looking for?" asked the ladybug. "Speak up!"

"Dolly!" said Baby Daisy, sadly.

"Dolly? Oh! You've lost your dolly? Well, maybe you left it outside. Follow me," said the ladybug, going out into the backyard.

The ladybug crept through the tall grass while Baby Daisy followed. They came to a dandelion and Baby Daisy grabbed its stem.

"Ouch!" squealed the dandelion. Baby Daisy fell back, startled.

"Don't stare! It's not polite!" scolded the dandelion.

The ladybug cleared her throat. "Tell me, Miss Dandelion, have you seen Baby Daisy's dolly?"

"No, but why don't you ask the flamingo?" said the dandelion. "He's taller than I, and can see more of the yard."

"Good idea," said the ladybug, and she led Baby Daisy through the grass until they reached the pretty pink plaster flamingo. Baby Daisy grabbed one of its skinny legs to pull herself up.

"Let go!" cried the flamingo. "Would you like it if I pulled on your leg like that?"

Baby Daisy shook her head.

"Oh, dear," said the ladybug, sighing. "Sorry to bother you, Mister Flamingo, but have you seen Baby Daisy's dolly?"

"I don't believe I have. But you might ask the rosebush. Her nose is very sensitive. Perhaps she can find Baby Daisy's dolly by sniffing."

"Thank you," said the ladybug. "Come, Baby Daisy. But please, don't touch anything else!"

Pretty soon they reached the rosebush and asked for her help.

"Sorry," said the rosebush sweetly. "But I don't smell anything out of the ordinary today. In fact, I'm not sure that dollies have a smell. Perhaps—stop, child!" she cried. Baby Daisy was about to prick her finger on a thorn.

"Now, as I was saying, I'll bet my petals that the tree can help you. He can see the entire back yard. He's sure to know where Baby Daisy's dolly is."

The ladybug thanked her and scurried over to the old oak by the garden shed.

"Why, yes!" said the tree when the ladybug asked about Daisy's dolly. "I can see it plain as day!" The tree pointed at the backyard fence. "It's there, by that patch of wild berries," he said.

Baby Daisy smiled and hurried over to the white wooden fence and the patch of wild berries.

"Dolly!" cried Baby Daisy happily. She lay down in the grass with the dolly beside her, and closed her eyes.

Baby Daisy drifted off to sleep. But when she awoke, she was in her bed, all alone, without her dolly.

Baby Daisy tumbled out of bed and went straight to the back yard. There, by the fence, near the patch of wild berries, was her dolly. Baby Daisy laughed. It was just like in the dream! Or was it?

Baby Daisy saw something on the tip of her dolly's nose. It was a ladybug! But before Baby Daisy could touch it, the ladybug spread her tiny wings and flew away.

If I Had a Dinosaur

If I had a dinosaur,
    He'd cause a lot of fuss
Every time I took him for
    A ride upon the bus.

If I had a dinosaur,
    He'd cause a big commotion
When I took him to the shore
    And bathed him in the ocean.

If I had a dinosaur,
    He'd be a nuisance, quite,
If he were the kind to snore
    In the middle of the night.

Castles in the Sand

It was a hot summer day. Baby Donald and his friends were at the beach. Baby Mickey was throwing a frisbee for Baby Pluto, while Baby Goofy and Baby Pete tossed a beach ball back and forth.

But Baby Donald was bored. He tried to think of something he could do by himself. Then he had an idea he would build a sandcastle!

Baby Donald grabbed his pail and shovel, and crawled to a spot where the sand was nice and damp. He dug up a handful of sand and started building one wall of the castle. When he thought the wall was high enough, he started on another.

It was hard, hot work, but Baby Donald kept on until the castle was finished. Then he sat back and smiled.

"Pretty!" thought Baby Donald. But it still seemed to be missing something.

"Shells!" Baby Donald thought to himself. He crawled off to see if he could find some.

But when he returned a few minutes later, his castle had disappeared!

Where could his sandcastle have gone? Baby Donald knew that his sandcastle didn't just walk away. Someone must have stolen it, he decided. But who?

Could it have been Baby Mickey?

Baby Donald found Baby Mickey still playing frisbee with Baby Pluto. Donald looked around, but there was no sign of his sandcastle anywhere. Baby Mickey hadn't taken it.

Baby Donald thought a minute. Maybe Baby Goofy had stolen his sandcastle.

Baby Donald found Baby Goofy collecting pretty shells and putting them in his pail. Baby Donald grabbed the pail and turned it upside down. He had made Baby Goofy cry, but he hadn't found his sandcastle. Baby Goofy hadn't taken it.

Baby Donald thought and thought. Maybe Baby Pete had stolen his sandcastle. It was just the sort of thing Baby Pete would do!

Baby Donald found Baby Pete at the end of the beach, chasing sand crabs. There were dozens of little mounds in the sand that the sand crabs had built, but there was no sign of Baby Donald's sandcastle. Baby Pete hadn't taken it.

Baby Donald couldn't think of anywhere else his sandcastle could be. He was sad for a whole minute. Then a smile spread across his face. If he could build one sandcastle, he could surely build another!

So that's just what he did. And when he had finished, he wanted the other Babies to see his lovely sandcastle. He was about to go get them when he saw Baby Mickey coming towards him.

"Look out!" said Baby Mickey, pointing. Baby Donald turned around just in time to see a big wave race up the shore to his sandcastle and knock it flat.

"No!" cried Baby Donald. In the blink of an eye, his second sandcastle was gone.

Baby Donald watched the waves roll away from the shore, and he knew that no one had stolen his sandcastle. Baby Donald knew that if he wanted a castle that wouldn't get washed away, he would have to build it differently.

Later, when it was time to go home, Baby Mickey, Baby Goofy, Baby Pete and Baby Pluto looked from one end of the beach to the other. And finally they found Baby Donald.

He was sitting proudly beside his new castle. He built it high up on the sand, far away from the waves. And this time, Baby Donald had built his castle out of rocks, seaweed, sand dollars, driftwood, shells—anything that he found on the beach. He had used some sand, as well, but only a little. He had built this castle to last! The other Disney Babies cheered.

When Baby Donald went home that day, he waved good-bye to his castle. He was a very tired Baby, but very, very happy.

The Sail-Away Day

Baby Mickey had a brand-new toy sail-boat, a red one with a white sail. He couldn't wait to take it to the small pond in the park and see how it would sail.

When Baby Mickey got to the pond, a friendly breeze was making little ripples in the water. What a wonderful day for sailing his boat!

Baby Donald, Baby Minnie and Baby Daisy were also at the pond, and they all had new sailboats, too. Baby Donald's boat was blue. Baby Minnie's boat was yellow. And Baby Daisy's boat was green. All of the sailboats had bright, white sails.

The four friends put their boats into the water and gave them each a little push. The sails caught the breeze and away they sailed.

"Yay!" shouted Baby Mickey.

"Yay!" shouted Baby Donald, Baby Minnie and Baby Daisy.

As Baby Mickey and his friends watched the four sailboats glide across the water, side by side, he hoped that his sailboat would reach the other side first.

When the boats were halfway across the little pond, the four Babies crawled to the other side and waited.

First a green sailboat reached the shore. It was Baby Daisy's boat.

Next a blue sailboat reached the shore. It was Baby Donald's boat.

Then another sailboat reached the shore. It was Baby Minnie's yellow boat.

Baby Mickey waited, but there was no red sailboat in sight. Baby Mickey wondered where it could be.

Baby Donald, Baby Minnie and Baby Daisy were all sorry that Baby Mickey's boat had not come to shore. They waited and waited. And waited some more.

Baby Mickey couldn't sail if he didn't have a boat. He had to sit and watch as his three friends put their boats into the water again and pushed them off.

As Baby Mickey watched the blue, green and yellow boats sail across the water, he suddenly saw something red!

"My boat," thought Baby Mickey. He looked a little closer at the red object. It *was* a red sailboat. Baby Pete was playing with it near the water's edge.

When Baby Pete saw Baby Mickey, he crawled away. Baby Mickey crawled after him. "Mine!" shouted Baby Mickey. He got closer and closer to Baby Pete.

Suddenly, Baby Pete stopped. He looked sadly at the red sailboat, then handed it over to Baby Mickey.

"Sorry," said Baby Pete.

Baby Mickey was surprised and happy to have his sailboat back. But he was not happy when Baby Pete burst into tears. He realized that Baby Pete didn't have a toy sailboat of his own.

"Come on," said Baby Mickey.

He and Baby Pete took the little red sailboat to the edge of the pond. Baby Pete gave it a push and away it sailed, pushed by a gentle breeze.

When the boat was halfway across the small pond, Baby Mickey and Baby Pete crawled to the other side and waited.

First, Baby Donald's blue sailboat reached the shore.

Next Baby Minnie's yellow sailboat reached the shore.

Then Baby Daisy's green sailboat reached the shore.

Finally the little red boat reached the shore.

"Yay!" Baby Mickey and Baby Pete yelled together.

For the rest of the afternoon, the five friends sailed their boats. Sometimes the blue boat came in first. Sometimes the green or yellow boat came in first. And sometimes, Baby Mickey's and Baby Pete's red boat came in first.

But no matter which boat came in first, all the Babies had a wonderful time, especially Baby Pete, who finally had a boat to sail, too.

Baby Brother

The stork brought baby brother.
It was a huge mistake!
I tried to send him back because
I knew he was a fake!

He cried and screamed forever!
I thought he'd never stop.
This can't be my kid brother—
He can't even skip, or hop!

Somebody please come get him!
He's pulling out my hair
And I can't even get back at him.
Somehow, it's not fair!

He's been here several days, now,
And I guess he's sort of fun.
But, please! Don't send another!
My hands are full with one!

The Tearful Teddy Bear

Baby Minnie sat in the middle of the floor, surrounded by toys and giggling with delight. There were cloth books and alphabet blocks, baby dolls and stuffed animals, a rattle and a jack-in-the-box.

Most of her toys were old, though, and today Baby Minnie wanted to play with her new ones. So she sorted through the toys and chose a new doll, a new hand puppet made of red and green felt, and a music box.

She lifted the top of the music box and let the sweet sound fill the room. Then she propped her dolly against one leg of the coffee table, and put on a show for her with the hand puppet.

Suddenly Baby Minnie heard a strange sound. What could it be?

Baby Minnie listened closely. It sounded like someone was crying! But who? And where?

Baby Minnie followed the sound to the bedroom. She looked behind the dresser. She looked on the windowsill. She looked underneath the bed. But she couldn't find the one who was making the sound.

Baby Minnie went to the toy chest and peered inside. But there was no sound coming from the wooden chest.

The only place left to look was the closet. Maybe the sound was coming from there.

The closet door swung open easily when she pushed it. She pushed past a white wicker hamper, several pairs of shoes, a single sneaker with missing laces, and a laundry basket full of fresh, clean clothes. The crying grew louder, and louder, and louder, until—

"Oh!" gasped Baby Minnie, startled. There, at the very back of the closet, stuck away in the corner, sat her old teddy bear. His brown fur was faded and worn, he was covered with a layer of dust, and tears were streaming down his fuzzy face.

Baby Minnie could hardly believe her eyes. Teddy Bear was crying!

Baby Minnie touched his fluffy cheek. "Bear!" said Minnie, glad to see her old friend. "Don't cry!"

"I can't help it," said Teddy Bear, tearfully. "You play with all the new toys, but you never play with me anymore." Teddy Bear sniffled loudly.

Baby Minnie knew it was true. She used to play with Teddy Bear all the time. He'd been her favorite toy for a long time, the one she never let anyone else play with.

But ever since her birthday, she had lots of different toys, and she'd forgotten all about him. In fact, she couldn't even remember when she'd put him in the closet.

But no matter how long he'd been there, Baby Minnie decided it was long enough.

She took Teddy Bear gently by the hand and led him out of the closet. She took him to the living room, pushed her new doll aside, and put Teddy Bear in its place. Then she wiped the tears from his black button eyes.

Baby Minnie lifted the top of the music box once again, and sang along with its tinkling melody. She picked up the hand puppet and, this time, she put on a show for her old friend, Teddy Bear.

Teddy Bear's fuzzy face lit up with a smile. He had his friend back!

When Baby Minnie took her nap that afternoon and snuggled beneath the covers, she made sure Teddy Bear was on the pillow right beside her!

At the Zoo

The kangaroo
Is always blue.
(He never, ever laughs.)

The same is true
Of the gloomy gnu
(And the serious giraffes).

The crocodile's
Not known for smiles.
(He couldn't look much meaner!)

The only one
Who's having fun
Is me (and the hyena)!

HYENA

The Amazing Magic Carpet Ride

Bang-bang-bang! Baby Gyro hammered away. Baby Gyro loved gears and wheels, he loved thingamabobs and whatchamacallits. In fact, Baby Gyro would rather have his rubber hammer and his bucket of nuts and bolts than all the teddy bears and wind-up toys in the world.

"Let's play!" said Baby Mickey. He and Baby Goofy were playing in Baby Gyro's yard. But they weren't interested in the old piece of torn carpeting and the funny painted ball Baby Gyro was tinkering with.

Clink, clank, clunk! Baby Gyro kept working while Baby Mickey and Baby Goofy played peek-a-boo.

After hammering away for a few more minutes, Baby Gyro waved at Baby Mickey and Baby Goofy, calling them over.

"Sit," said Baby Gyro. Baby Mickey and Baby Goofy sat on the carpet, next to the painted ball.

"Fly! Fly!" shouted Baby Gyro, and he spun the funny painted ball. Suddenly, the carpet rose up in the air and began to fly.

"Whooaa!" yelled Baby Mickey and Baby Goofy, hanging on tightly.

Soon, Baby Mickey, Baby Goofy and Baby Gyro were flying high above the earth on the magic carpet. It was fun looking down at the little buildings and even littler people, until the rug swooped down and landed on top of an ice-covered mountain.

"Hold on!" said Baby Gyro as the carpet slid down the mountainside.

"Wheee!" shouted Baby Mickey and Baby Goofy.

The carpet landed on a large, flat block of ice on the bank of a river. There was a large *crack!* and the ice began to move. Soon they were riding toward a huge waterfall!

"Fly!" shouted Baby Goofy.

Baby Gyro spun the painted ball. Soon, the magic carpet rose into the air again.

After a while, the magic carpet dove down and landed at the feet of a huge statue in the middle of a sandy desert. The statue had the body of a lion and the head of a man. It was called the Sphinx.

"Hello," said Baby Gyro as the Magic Carpet slid down the Sphinx's nose.

But before the Sphinx could answer, the wind began to blow, and a thick cloud of sand swirled up. Soon it was impossible to see anything.

"Fly!!" said Baby Mickey, coughing.

Baby Gyro spun the globe once more and the magic carpet took off. Below them, Baby Goofy watched the green land change to blue sea.

"Water!" said Baby Goofy. *Whoosh!* The Magic Carpet spun down and landed on a large gray island But they were still moving, because the island turned out to be the back of a happy whale.

Baby Gyro and his friends sailed on the back of the whale for a long time. Then there was a huge splash as a fountain of water sprayed out of the top of the whale, sending the magic carpet straight up in the air.

"Fly!" said Baby Mickey, spinning the globe round and round. The carpet rose into the air.

"Fly!" said Baby Goofy, spinning the globe round and round. The carpet rose higher.

"Fly! Fly!" said Baby Gyro, spinning the globe faster and faster. The carpet flew higher yet.

Suddenly, the Magic Carpet bucked and rolled. It had gone high enough. It took a dive, heading straight for Baby Gyro's yard, where it landed smoothly and safely.

"Shame on you babies," scolded Gyro's mother. "You shouldn't be playing with my best rug!"

She took the carpet in the house. Baby Mickey and Baby Goofy felt sad. But Baby Gyro grabbed his hammer and his bucket of nuts and bolts and crawled over to a stack of boards near the house.

"Here!" said Baby Gyro. "Rocket ship!"

"Fly! Fly!" shouted Baby Mickey and Baby Goofy.

Snow

Snow can be green,
    Snow can be pink.
Snow can be purple
    (My favorite, I think).

Snow can be colored
    Like fresh apricots.
Snow can have stripes,
    Or round polka-dots.

Where is this snow
    With the colorful look?
You'll find it right here
    In my coloring book!

Lights Out!

Baby Donald was spending the night at Baby Mickey's house. Baby Goofy and Baby Pluto were there, too. They all played together in Baby Mickey's room, but once the sun went down, it was time to go to bed.

"No!" said Baby Donald. He did not want to go to bed. He might miss something while he slept. Besides, Baby Donald didn't like the dark.

But it was late, and the babysitter tucked them all in for the night. "Sleep well," she said. Then she turned out the light and slipped out of the room, closing the door behind her.

"Night," said Baby Mickey and Baby Goofy.

"Night," said Baby Donald.

"Yip, yip!" barked Baby Pluto.

Soon they were all fast asleep.

Sometime later, Baby Donald woke up. He looked around the darkened room. There were shadows everywhere, and Baby Donald was afraid. He held on to his blanket tightly, trying not to cry.

"Home," thought Baby Donald, and he slipped out of bed and started crawling towards the door.

Suddenly he bumped into a wall. He sat back on the rug and rubbed his head. When he was sure he was okay, Baby Donald started off again.

Baby Donald's hand came down on something round and rubber. It rolled, and again he went tumbling.

Baby Donald was frightened. What could have made him fall? Baby Donald didn't know that it was Baby Mickey's red rubber ball. He couldn't see it in the dark.

Baby Donald again started to feel his way across the room. Soon he ran into something big, and stiff, and fuzzy.

Baby Donald scrambled away as fast as he could. He had bumped into Baby Mickey's giant stuffed tiger. But Baby Donald couldn't see what it was in the dark. To him, it felt like a monster.

Carefully, Baby Donald once again tried to make his way out. He could see light from the hallway, shining in underneath the door. Just a little bit farther and he would be there!

Then Baby Donald touched something that felt like a round metal pole. He wrapped his fingers around it and pulled himself up. Holding on to it, Baby Donald took a few baby steps, then fell against something stringy. He pushed against the something, but his hand went right through it and got caught. Baby Donald pulled and pulled, but he couldn't get his hand free.

Baby Donald plopped down on the floor and started to cry. He didn't know that the something was the net around Baby Mickey's playpen. All he knew was that it wouldn't let him go home.

Suddenly Baby Donald felt something warm and wet brush up and down his cheek. He tried to push the warm, wet thing away. Then something cold and hard poked him in the face. Now he was really frightened.

Baby Donald didn't know that the warm, wet thing was Baby Pluto's tongue. And the cold, hard thing was Baby Pluto's nose!

Suddenly, the door opened and the light came on. "What's going on in here?" the babysitter asked.

Baby Donald looked around the room. He saw Mickey's ball, and the stuffed tiger, and the wall that he had bumped into, and the play-pen net he was stuck in. Then he saw Baby Mickey and Baby Goofy in bed, and Baby Pluto on the floor. They were all awake now.

Baby Donald stopped crying. He felt silly, now that the light was on and he knew there was nothing in Baby Mickey's room to be afraid of.

"All right," said the babysitter. "Back to bed you go."

Baby Donald lay in bed, smiling. The room was dark and there were shadows everywhere. But Baby Donald was not afraid. He knew that the dark really wasn't scary, after all.

Little Me

Little fingers,
      Little toes,
Two bright eyes,
      One small nose!

Put them together
      Carefully,
And what you've got
      Is little me!

Lullaby to a Bear

Go to sleep, my teddy bear!
I've sung a dozen lullabyes!
But all you do is sit and stare,
And never close your button eyes!

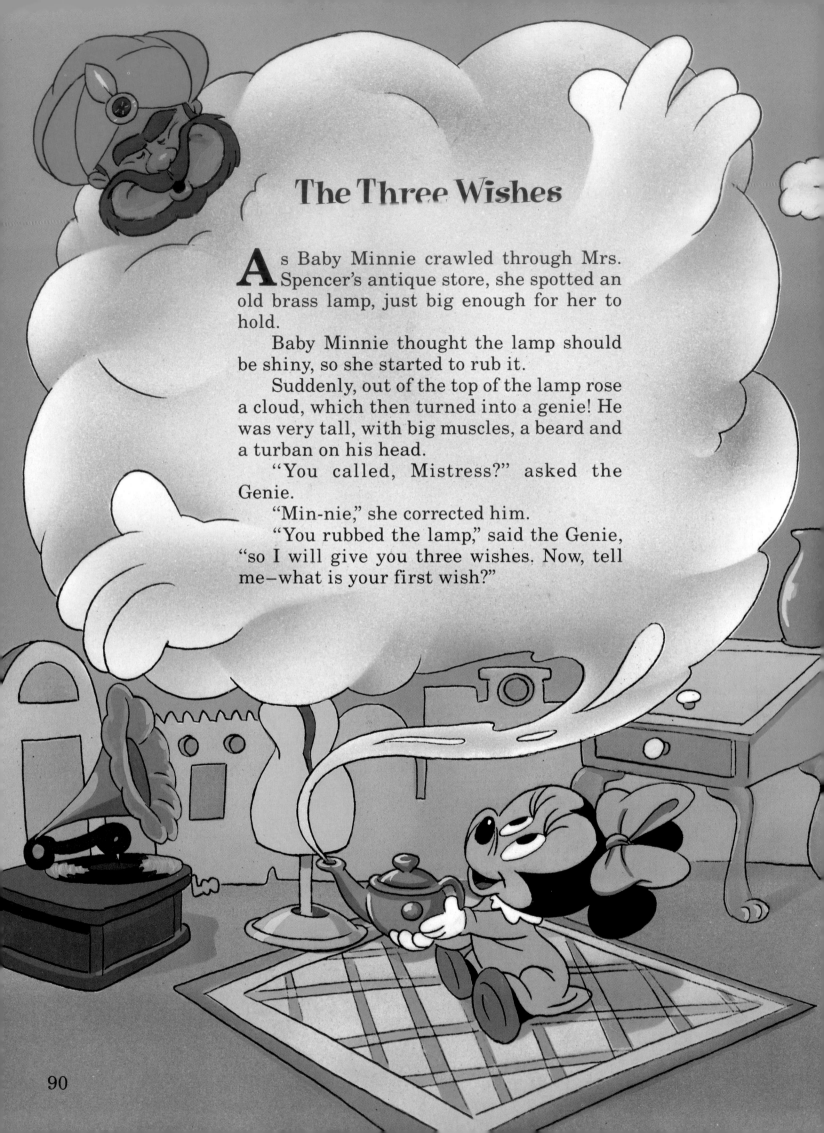

The Three Wishes

As Baby Minnie crawled through Mrs. Spencer's antique store, she spotted an old brass lamp, just big enough for her to hold.

Baby Minnie thought the lamp should be shiny, so she started to rub it.

Suddenly, out of the top of the lamp rose a cloud, which then turned into a genie! He was very tall, with big muscles, a beard and a turban on his head.

"You called, Mistress?" asked the Genie.

"Min-nie," she corrected him.

"You rubbed the lamp," said the Genie, "so I will give you three wishes. Now, tell me—what is your first wish?"

Baby Minnie thought for a second. "Ice cream!" she cried.

"Your wish is my command," said the Genie.

Suddenly Baby Minnie felt very cold, and when she looked around, she wasn't in the antique store anymore. She was in the middle of a cold, icy land.

"Brrr!" said Baby Minnie.

She looked around again. That wasn't snow on the ground, after all. It was vanilla ice cream! There was a river of chocolate syrup running down a strawberry mountain, and in the lake below floated puffs of whipped cream.

Baby Minnie wasn't in a land of ice, she was smack dab in the middle of the world's biggest ice-cream sundae!

But she couldn't find the cherry, which was Baby Minnie's favorite part of the sundae. "Up on top," said the Genie. And, sure enough, on top of the huge strawberry-ice-cream mountain, was a bright red cherry.

Baby Minnie tried to crawl up the mountain, but she kept sliding down. Soon she was too cold even to think about ice cream.

"Does Mistress Baby Minnie want her second wish?" asked the Genie.

Baby Minnie nodded her head. "Toys!" she shouted.

Suddenly, Baby Minnie felt warm again. She found herself in the window of a toy store, surrounded by toys of every shape and size. A charming tune was coming from a silver music box.

"Come dance with me," said a beautiful ballerina, spinning around on top of the music box. Baby Minnie spun round and round, too, until she was dizzy.

"Ooh!" giggled Baby Minnie.

"Can you do this?" a friendly voice called out. Baby Minnie turned and saw a toy acrobat hanging from his knees on a trapeze and swinging back and forth, back and forth.

"No!" laughed Baby Minnie.

"Out of the way! Time for our drill!" a gruff voice commanded.

TOYS

Tramp, tramp, tramp! A long line of wooden soldiers marched past Baby Minnie. "Halt!" called their captain.

The soldiers stopped marching and saluted Baby Minnie. She saluted right back.

"Watch out!" A fuzzy bear rolled by, balancing on a ball. Baby Minnie clapped and giggled.

Tap, tap, tap! Someone was tapping at the glass. It was a little girl who was looking in the window of the toy store. "I'll take that one," said the little girl, pointing right at Baby Minnie. "I want to take her home."

Baby Minnie stopped laughing. Even though the little girl looked very nice, Baby Minnie thought she'd rather go to her own house.

"You have one more wish, Mistress," said the Genie.

Baby Minnie thought for a moment. "Back!" she said.

In a flash, Baby Minnie was back in the antique store, holding the old lamp. There was no genie in sight.

"Would you like to buy that lamp?" said Mrs. Spencer, who owned the store.

Baby Minnie shook her head and handed the lamp back to Mrs. Spencer. "They say this lamp can grant wishes. What do you wish for, Baby Minnie?" Mrs. Spencer asked.

"Home!" said Baby Minnie, climbing into her stroller.

Sharing

"It's mine!" I said.
My face turned red
    When Daisy grabbed my choo-choo.

"I will not share.
I do not care
    If you scream 'til you're quite blue!"

She went away.
She wouldn't stay.
    She crawled under a table.

Then I gave in.
I just can't win!
    I guess I'm just not able.

She played awhile.
I saw her smile.
    She brought the choo-choo my way.

Sharing's not bad.
I guess I'm glad
    That both of us can play.

The Playful Pup

If Baby Pluto had been able to tell time, he would have known it was two o'clock in the afternoon. He would have known why he couldn't find anyone to play with. He would have known that Baby Mickey was taking a nap. Baby Mickey took a nap every afternoon at two o'clock. But, like most puppies, Baby Pluto couldn't tell time. So he didn't know why he didn't have anyone to play with. He just knew he didn't.

Baby Pluto didn't have a special time to take naps. He just took them when he felt like it. Right now, he didn't feel like napping, he felt like playing.

Baby Pluto decided that he'd just have to look for somebody to play with.

So off Baby Pluto went, bounding down the street as fast as his puppy legs could carry him.

Pretty soon a boy on a bicycle stopped and played with Baby Pluto for a few minutes. But the boy was delivering newspapers, and couldn't stay to play longer.

When the boy pedaled off, Baby Pluto chased him. But the bicycle went too fast for the little puppy.

Baby Pluto stopped chasing the bicycle and sat down to catch his breath. He was on a strange new street. Baby Pluto looked around and saw that he was sitting near the entrance to what looked like a park.

As all puppies know, there's always someone to play with in a park. With a happy bark, Baby Pluto dashed through the entrance, under the fancy ironwork letters that said "Zoo."

Even if Baby Pluto had been able to read the sign, he still wouldn't have known where he was. He had never been to a zoo before.

So you can imagine how surprised and delighted he was to find so many different animals to play with.

Baby Pluto wriggled through the fence and ran over to where a seal was playing. Now, the seal's house was pretty damp, because when seals play, they play in a big pool of water. Before he knew it, Baby Pluto was soggier than a doggy liked to be.

Playing with the seal wasn't as much fun as he'd thought it would be. So Baby Pluto said good-bye to the seal and ran over to see the giraffe. The giraffe was happy to see Baby Pluto, and was eager to play. But she had such a long neck and such long legs that she couldn't see the little puppy, and she kept stepping on his tail.

Playing with the giraffe wasn't as much fun as he'd thought it would be. So Baby Pluto said good-bye to the giraffe and went to find someone else to play with.

"Someone else" turned out to be a baby goat. But the goat's favorite game was butting Baby Pluto with his forehead. When he grew up, the baby goat would butt with his horns instead of his forehead, but, lucky for Baby Pluto, the goat didn't have horns yet.

Playing with the goat wasn't as much fun as he'd thought it would be. So Baby Pluto said good-bye to the goat and went to find someone else to play with.

This time, he ran to the elephant's house. The elephant wanted to play his favorite game: squirting water through his trunk. So he filled up his trunk with water and squirted Baby Pluto right in the face.

Baby Pluto had already been wet once this afternoon, and that was enough. He'd had just about enough play, too.

Baby Pluto ran out of the zoo and, after taking a few wrong turns, finally found his way home. Baby Mickey was awake and waiting to play with him.

Baby Pluto was glad to be home, but he was very tired. Before he could play with Baby Mickey, he had to take a nap. And as he fell asleep, he thought that, from now on, he'd stick to playing with someone his own size!

Baby Talk

Sometimes I look
    Like I'm happy.
And sometimes I look
    Like I'm not.
In words, I can't say
    How I'm feeling today.
But my face always tells you
    What's what!

A Pussycat Tale

When my little kitty sees
Me upon my hands and knees,
I wonder if she's thinking that
I'm another kitty cat!

An Afternoon in the Park

One day, when it was especially warm and sunny outside, Baby Mickey and Baby Donald rode to the park in their strollers.

"Go!" said Baby Mickey.

"Faster!" said Baby Donald.

The park was their favorite place to go, because there were lots of trees and flowers there. There was a pond, too, with tiny fish, bullfrogs, and small turtles. And, best of all, there was a playground with lots of fun things to do.

When they got to the park, Baby Mickey and Baby Donald couldn't decide what to do first. Should they play in the sandbox? Or climb up on the seesaw? Or ride down the slide?

Baby Mickey looked over at the giant slide. It stood in the center of the playground, looking silvery in the sunlight.

"No," said Mickey, shaking his head. He was a little afraid of the slide. He always went down too fast, and sometimes he fell off the end, right into the sand. He didn't like that very much. Should they toss their ball first? Or go on the swings? There were so many different things to do!

Baby Mickey started off in the direction of the seesaws.

"No!" cried Baby Donald, trying to pull Baby Mickey the other way.

"Let go!" said Baby Mickey. Baby Donald always wanted to have his own way, and Baby Mickey didn't like that.

Baby Mickey finally pulled his hand free. He looked down at the red ball by his feet and offered it to Baby Donald. But Baby Donald pointed to the sandbox. He wanted to play there first, so he grabbed the pail from Baby Mickey, and tried to snatch the shovel as well.

"No!" yelled Baby Mickey. He held on to the shovel tightly and pushed Baby Donald away.

Baby Donald was very, very angry, and so was Baby Mickey. Each one decided to play by himself.

Baby Donald crawled into the sandbox, dragging the pail behind him. He set the pail down in the sand and started to fill it with his hands. But the sand ran out through his fingers, and the pail wasn't getting full. How would he get the sand into the pail? Baby Donald was not having any fun in the sandbox. He decided to try the swings instead.

When Baby Donald found the swings, he saw that Baby Mickey was already there. But Baby Mickey didn't look like he was having much fun, either. He was just sitting in the swing, kicking his legs back and forth, trying to make it go. But he could only make the swing move a little from side to side.

Baby Mickey wished he had someone to push him. He liked to feel the cool breeze touch his face. But there was no one to push him, because he and Baby Donald were mad at each other.

Baby Donald decided to try the seesaw, but when he climbed up on one end of the seesaw, it just dropped to the ground.

"Ouch!" cried Baby Donald. He slid off of the seesaw, rubbing his hurt bottom.

Poor Baby Donald. If he had someone to sit on the other end, then he could ride the seesaw up and down. But he couldn't ride the seesaw all alone. Baby Donald sighed.

Baby Mickey decided to play with his red ball. He threw it up in the air, and caught it. Then he threw it up in the air and caught it again. After a while, Baby Mickey was bored. Playing ball all by himself was no fun. He needed someone to toss it to, and someone who would toss it back. But there was no one. Unless...

Baby Mickey went looking for Baby Donald. And at that very moment, Baby Donald was on his way to find Baby Mickey. When they met at the sandbox, they frowned at each other. Baby Mickey started laughing, then Baby Donald joined him. Together, they climbed into the sandbox.

Baby Donald set the pail down between them, and Baby Mickey pulled out the shovel.

They played in the warm sand for a while. Then they went to the swings, and took turns pushing each other. Then they went to the seesaw, and rode up and down. After a while, they tossed the red ball back and forth. "This is fun!" thought Baby Donald and Baby Mickey.

By the end of the day, Baby Mickey and Baby Donald had forgotten all about being angry. They both had a good time, after all. But having so much fun had made them tired! So when Baby Donald and Baby Mickey got home, they went right to sleep.

My Silly Friend

I have a silly friend I see
    At night above my head.
He always comes to play with me
    When I'm tucked up in my bed.

And so I sleep the whole night through,
    Until the light of day.
But then, the moon, my silly friend,
    Goes home to sleep all day!

The Baby
and the Beanstalk

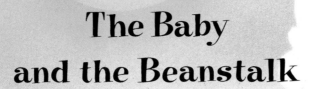

Once upon a time, there was a Baby who liked to grow things. His name was Baby Goofy. One day Baby Goofy found some seeds. He didn't know what kind of seeds they were, but he thought he'd plant them and see what came up.

So Baby Goofy dug a hole with his little shovel. Then he put the seeds in the hole, covered them up, and worked the soil with his toy hoe. Finally, he watered the soil with his watering can.

Baby Goofy lay down on his tummy, and propped his head in his hand, and watched.

And, sure enough, a fat vine began to grow from the spot where he had planted his seeds. The fat vine became a tall vine, so tall that the top of it disappeared into the clouds.

"Ooooh! Big," said Baby Goofy, looking up, up, up at the leafy green plant. He wished he were big enough to climb it. But he didn't have to wish for long, for soon a big green leaf reached out and slid underneath him.

"Go up!" said Baby Goofy. Like an elevator, the leaf rose, carrying Baby Goofy up into the clouds.

There he discovered a strange land, where everything was very, very large—especially a big stone house. It began to rain, but, lucky for Baby Goofy, the door to the house was open. He hurried inside.

"Gawrsh!" thought Baby Goofy, looking around. Everything was so big—giant tables, giant chairs, a giant fireplace, even giant cups and saucers. Baby Goofy wondered if a giant person lived there, too.

Suddenly he heard giant foot-steps, so loud they shook the walls. Baby Goofy crawled into a giant slipper near the fireplace and hid.

"Fee - fie - foo - fout! Stranger among us, come on out!" rumbled a giant voice.

Baby Goofy gulped, crawling out of the slipper.

"Hi," he said in a squeaky voice, sounding as if he had a cold.

The giant was as tall as Baby Goofy's own house! "Fee-fie-fiddle-dee-diddle! Answer me this giant riddle! What kind of bow is it that can't be tied or untied?" demanded the giant.

Baby Goofy scratched his head. He was afraid the giant might be mad if he didn't know the answer. He reached back and touched the tie on the back of his bib. It was shaped in a bow.

"Bow?" said Baby Goofy.

"Wrong!" The giant cups and saucers clattered as the giant voice roared out. Outside, the rain still poured down.

"Think, little baby! Think!" the giant said.

Baby Goofy thought and thought, but he still had no answer. He looked at the door longingly, then up at the giant. "Home!" said Baby Goofy.

"Not until you answer my riddle, little baby," the giant replied.

Baby Goofy frowned, then looked out the window, thinking of his room, his toys, and all his friends. Outside, it had stopped raining. Not only that, but a rainbow had appeared in the sky.

"Rainbow!" said Baby Goofy, pointing at the beautiful sight.

"That's it, little baby!" laughed the giant. "A rainbow can't be tied or untied! You answered the riddle!"

Then he picked up Baby Goofy and bounced him on his giant knee. He was a pretty nice giant, after all.

After cookies and cocoa, Baby Goofy asked the giant, "Go home?"

"Sure enough," said the giant. "But I'll miss you, little baby."

So the giant carried Baby Goofy out of his house and down the vine. Then, after shaking his hand, he climbed back up the vine and disappeared into the clouds, pulling the vine back up again.

Baby Goofy crawled towards his house, but he was so busy looking back at the vine as the giant pulled it up into the sky, that he bumped right into his door.

"Oof!" said Baby Goofy. He sure felt silly, always bumping into things. But he didn't think about that for long, because he looked up in the sky and once again saw that wonderful band of color.

"Rainbow!" said Baby Goofy. It was exactly the kind of bow that couldn't be tied or untied.

Goodbye

And now it's time to say goodbye
To you, our favorite friend.
We're sure you know the reason why—
Because this is...THE END!